RICHTON PARK PUBLIC LIBRARY DISTRICT

3 6087 0   W9-BDG-929   R

YOU ARE RESPONSIBLE
FOR ANY DAMAGE AT
TIME OF RETURN

Daphne, Secret Vlogger

Daphne, Secret Vlogger is published by Stone Arch Books
A Capstone Imprint
1710 Roe Crest Drive
North Mankato, Minnesota 56003
www.mycapstone.com

Copyright © 2019 Capstone

All rights reserved. No part of this publication may be reproduced in whole
or in part, or stored in a retrieval system, or transmitted in any form or by
any means, electronic, mechanical, photocopying, recording, or otherwise,
without written permission of the publisher.

Library of Congress Cataloging-in-Publication Data is available on the
Library of Congress website.

Summary: Ridiculous makeup, blinding spotlights, and too much catty
drama! Annabelle Daphne Louis starts her second assignment from her
therapist to venture outside of her comfort zone at her new school. This
time, she's trying her hand at theater. Failing the auditions for *Little Shop of
Horrors*, Annabelle finds her place backstage. But when Annabelle features
some funny impersonations on her vlog, *Daphne Doesn't*, the drama is just
beginning. When the play director shares Daphne's videos with the cast,
Annabelle starts experiencing some real-life drama. And as her likes and
followers increase like crazy, Annabelle begins to realize that it doesn't mean
anything if she doesn't have the guts to make friends in real life.

ISBN 978-1-4965-6295-1 (library-bound hardcover)
ISBN 978-1-4965-6299-9 (paperback)
ISBN 978-1-4965-6303-3 (eBook PDF)

Cover illustration by Marcos Calo
Design by Kay Fraser

Printed and bound in Canada
PA020

DAPHNE
Definitely
DOESN'T DO
DRAMA

by Tami Charles

STONE ARCH BOOKS
a capstone imprint

1

SAME NIGHTMARE

Being famous isn't easy, especially when you're a rising YouTube star. Take this morning, for example. Beyoncé's "Run the World (Girls)" is blasting as my limo pulls up to McManus Middle School. Crowds are gathered around my hot ride, cameras out, ready to take selfies with *me*. But first, a girl's gotta apply a coat of bubblegum lip gloss and run a brush through her hair. My chauffeur gets out of the driver's seat, comes around, and opens my door. And the fans go WILD! Lights are flashing. Kids are shouting:

"Can I have your autograph, Daphne?"

"You're so cool!"

"Sit at my table at lunch, please?"

"But of course!" I say in my best British accent.

The girls are crying. The boys are drooling. And I am loving every. Single. Second.

I've got this whole "new kid at school" thing down pat.

Then again, maybe not.

Because the clouds begin to move in, blocking the sun. Then, a loud crack echoes across the sky. The rain comes down in sheets. My perfectly styled hair gets drenched. My trendy, straight-off-the-runway outfit morphs into my typical: shabby not-so-chic. Everyone is laughing, snorting, pointing—you know how this goes. Next comes the evil witch laughter sound effect, followed by a piercing scream.

AHHHHH!

My alarm goes off. Dream over. Back to

being Annabelle Louis, the Air Force brat from Germany—not Daphne. Back to being the new kid at McManus who no one really notices, except for like three people. Dork by day. YouTube vlogger by night. It's like I'm a living, breathing double agent. I jolt upright, see myself in my dresser mirror, and yep, it's me. Same frizzy hair. Same dorky everything. Same living nightmare.

2

HOT STUFF

If I'm being totally honest, this undercover vlogger gig does have me feeling like hot stuff . . . sometimes. Two hundred subscribers and counting? And who wouldn't love reading comments like these:

"You're so cool, Daphne!"

"Keep the vlogs coming!"

And the best one yet:

"I wish you went to my school."

Personally, I wish I went to NO school! At least not *real* school with actual human beings. I didn't have to when we lived on base overseas. Why mess up a good thing now?

The girl that people see on the YouTube screen, Daphne, isn't really me. The real me is a potential seventh-grade dropout. A computer dork who'd rather be locked in her basement "girl cave" all day. Who'd rather still be living in Germany, or even better, the UK, and homeschooled by her dad.

But *noooo*!

My parents just had to move us to Linden, New Jersey, and send me to a therapist, Dr. Varma, after Mom broke the news that the Air Force was sending her to Afghanistan on TDY—temporary duty yonder. So naturally Dr. Varma got all "therapisty" on me and suggested I make a vlog so I can "try new activities at school to make new friends and cope with Mom leaving." And my parents and best friend, Mae, all seemed to agree with her! Next thing I knew, I was making a fool of myself during Sports Day at school and then going undercover to post about it on YouTube. *Daphne Definitely Doesn't Do Sports* got a load of views and they were all like, *Omg, you're gonna go viral!* Now everyone expects me to keep this social experiment going.

Next up: DRAMA. Whereupon I'll audition for the school play, embarrass myself, and then go home and vlog about how this was yet another waste of time. Take that, Dr. Varma!

So here I am dragging myself to tryouts for *Little Shop of Horrors*. The title is fitting—middle school really is a place of horror.

The drama director, Mr. Davis, is passing out scripts when I get to the auditorium. I take one and go *wayyyy* in the back of the auditorium to sit—the very last row. I consider texting Mae and telling her I quit before I even started. But it's six hours ahead in the UK, and she's probably sleeping. And even if she weren't, I already know what she'd say: This is easy Annabelle! Just do it!

In theory, this all sounds easy. Read a few lines. Do a couple of simple dances. Sing a tune.

John, my first McManus friend, spots me in the back of the auditorium and rushes my way. Sometimes I wonder if he has sniff detectors the way he always seems to find me. "What happened to the cow who auditioned for the play?" he asks.

"I don't know," I say.

"He got *mooed* off stage." John laughs, and I can't help but do the same. Clairna, McManus friend #2, rolls her eyes as she walks over to us.

Mr. Davis rings a bell to get everyone's attention. "Ladies and gentlemen, please take a seat in the first couple of rows. We are about to get started with our auditions!"

I let out a sigh and trail behind John to the front: shoulders caved, feet slow-dragging against the floor, praying no one is looking at me. Meanwhile John is skipping and snapping down the aisle, to which Mr. Davis cheerfully says, "That's the spirit!"

He calls the boys up to the stage first. He reviews some "simple" dance moves. Four grapevines, four turn-claps, and for the finishing touch, a fist-pump leap toward the sky. *Easy enough,* I think. Then he reviews a short verse of "Suddenly Seymour" and has all the boys sing along. Next, he calls up the girls to do the same.

You might think this part is easy because there's a group of us, all braving the stage together. But did I mention how much I LOATHE doing anything in a group?

I tuck myself in the back line and move through the dance steps. It appears that all of my limbs are on strike today. The other students move together in sync. And I am crashing into girls left and right.

One of those girls happens to be Rachael, "Queen of Seventh Grade," and she's in the row ahead of mine.

The first time I bump into her, she doesn't say anything. Just turns around and gives me a look mad enough to melt my face off. It's the third kick in her ankles that sends hot fire spewing from her mouth: "I hope you don't call this dancing! You need to get your whole life together, girl!"

It feels like someone punches me in the gut. Hard. Somebody, anybody, get me out of here!

The girls around us start laughing. I stop "dancing." Clairna gives me a reassuring look. Finally, I catch up on the last three counts, in time to hit the last pose.

Thankfully, Mr. Davis calls us all back to our seats. But then he announces he'll be calling us up in twos to read lines from the script.

First up is John, who's paired with Rachael. The whole time they read their lines, my eyes are glued to John. He nails it. John is a living, breathing Seymour Krelborn! From the scruffy hair and the wire-framed glasses, right down to his penny loafers!

The music begins. Rachael and John begin to sing and dance. Rachael dances flawlessly. She doesn't miss one step. John tries to keep up with her, always moving half a beat behind her, but for some strange reason, it works. And they sound great singing together. Usually John doesn't get much attention, but when their scene is over, everyone claps really loud.

"John, your voice is as lovely as your trumpet playing!" Mr. Davis says.

"I'm what they call a triple threat," John responds, and takes a bow.

Mr. Davis calls up the next group. After John and Rachael's performance, I'm almost certain it's time to leave. So while the kids on stage perform, I grab my knapsack and start tiptoeing toward the exit.

But they finish quicker than expected. Everyone claps, and Mr. Davis says: "Next up, Annabelle Louis and Austin Coleman."

Busted. Again.

Everyone turns to look at me. My shoulders slump into a pile of mush. I pull the folded script out of my pocket, place my knapsack on a chair, and make my way to the stage. I can feel the entire world staring at me.

Austin is already standing on stage by the time my legs finally decide to get there. I should probably mention that Austin Coleman is music-video, basketball-dribbling cute.

Mr. Davis starts the music. I take a deep breath and try my best to pretend I'm Daphne, the popular YouTube vlogger. Minus the cameras and the cool British accent. *I can do this, I can do this*, I tell myself.

But four counts in, I'm already having a hard time keeping up with Austin—who, might I add, is now officially dance-star cute. He goes left, I go right. Not one move is coordinated, and I can't find a way to control my spaghetti arms and legs, even though my mind is screaming at my body to do what Austin is doing. How can dancing be this hard?

He sings the first line of "Suddenly Seymour," and when I join him, in harmony, things start to seem better. No one is laughing, so that's good. I'm coasting through the lower notes, voice smooth as a baby's bottom. I start to really get into it too. Close my eyes. Picture myself singing in front of millions of screaming fans. Hello, Daphne, and goodbye, Annabelle! But then I go for the high note. It comes out in the key of squeal.

And cue theme music to Jaws!

My voice cracks, and somehow the note I was supposed to hit morphs into something like a call to the wild.

Eyes open. Mouth drops. Soul crushed. I could have done much better if I was alone in the one space where I truly feel myself—in my girl cave, just me and my camera.

Mr. Davis scrambles to cut off the music.

"Let's move on to the script," he says nervously.

John gives me a thumbs-up from the audience even though I know I just blew it.

Austin and I start to read back and forth, this time no dancing and no singing. By the second line, I don't even need the script anymore. I've seen this show so many times, I could probably recite the lines backward. Thirty more seconds of this horror show, and I'm done.

"Great job, you two!" Mr. Davis says as Austin and I exit the stage, but I know he's lying.

When auditions are over, Mr. Davis leads everyone in a round of applause.

"Everyone was excellent! I'll announce the cast tomorrow, so stay tuned. In the meantime, I'll pass around a list for behind-the-scenes activities, so be sure to add your name if you'd like to volunteer."

By the time I get the list, I notice the lines for stage crew are empty. Maybe I should do that? It's better than embarrassing myself in front of a whole audience. Then at least I can satisfy Dr. Varma's request to participate in extracurricular activities.

For some reason, my inner Daphne voice takes over and says: *There's no way you'd embarrass yourself.* But of course I don't listen. I add my name, pass the list to John, and throw away any thoughts of being in the spotlight. Even if it did feel good for a millisecond when I was singing.

After the way today's auditions turned out, I'm convinced that this drama stuff is not my cup of tea.

3

THE RESULTS

Mr. Davis makes an announcement over the loudspeaker the next morning. "Will everyone who auditioned for *Little Shop of Horrors* report to the auditorium during seventh period? Late passes will be given out. Our meeting will be brief."

I spend the whole day nervous about the play. Meanwhile, by the time I get to my locker at the end of the day, YouTube notifications have blown up my phone. Over three thousand views

for "Daphne Definitely Doesn't Do Sports."
And fifteen hundred views for my second video
about school lunch! Wow!

John catches me looking at my own video for
like the fiftieth time. "Someone's obsessed," he
says.

There's a yank in my stomach. I turn the
screen off and slip my phone into my knapsack.
"No, not at all," I say. Then I add, "She's OK, I
guess."

"She's hilarious. Actually, I think you kinda
look like her." He flashes me a smile so wide
that his dimple sinks deep into his cheek.

And then my stomach starts doing this little
wave thing again.

"How do you think you did in the audition?"
he asks.

"Ha!" I laugh. "I was probably the worst one
up on that stage."

John shakes his head. "Nope! I think you're
in!"

Just then I see Rachael and company at

the popular table, smack in the middle of the cafeteria where everyone can notice her. She must *feel* me staring. And I don't know why I am. But I half-wave, half-smile, like some helpless puppy waiting for my fur-ever family to *Pick me! Pick me!*

For a split second, it looks like she wants to return the smile, rescue me from the entrapment of dorkdom, crown me equally as popular as her. But then, her whole face changes. Like she remembers the number of times I kicked and bumped into her yesterday. That's when she gives me a major eye-roll and returns her attention to those who matter most: her loyal subjects.

The seventh-period bell rings, and we head to the auditorium.

Mr. Fingerlin, the school counselor, is in the hallway as we walk by. "Annabelle, your mom told me you were trying out for the play!" He's totally excited. "It's great to see you settling in so fast."

I flash Mr. Fingerlin my best smile, knowing that if I don't say something pleasant, he'll go texting mom. They go way back to their Air Force days.

"Sure thing. Mr. Fingerlin. I'm fitting in just great."

LIES!!! My inner voice cries out.

I'm not sure how much I'm fitting in at a new school with hundreds of students and only three friends: John, Clairna, and Navdeep. The jury is still out on how real these friendships are. But they did take pity on me when I completely embarrassed myself in front of everyone on Sports Day.

John asks, "If you're not into drama, why'd you try out?"

I almost say "my therapist," but then I stop myself. Because what if he thinks it's weird that I go to therapy? But saying "my mom made me do it" would sound just as lame, so I just go with, "I wanted to try something new."

At least it's half true.

"What are you into, then? I mean . . . since drama is new to you?"

"Computers. I'm a techie."

"Yes, I remember your first day of school when I caught your backpack and your MacBook almost fell out."

"And that's why I don't want to bring it anymore," I joke.

Mr. Davis is waiting in the auditorium with tons of boxes on the stage. "Settle down, everyone!" he says. "Come in and take a seat." He pulls out a sheet of paper. "I'm happy to report that everyone did a great job yesterday— all thirty-one of you."

Everyone starts clapping and cheering.

"And because I think that drama is an art form all students should experience, I have decided to include *all* of you in the play."

Everybody jumps up and claps. I stand up too, slowly realizing that holy goodness, I'm in a play. And suddenly, I don't know how to feel. Happy? "Lit"? Scared? Or all of the above?

D. Final answer.

John leans over and says, "Told you Mr. Davis was cool like that!"

"OK, take a seat," Mr. Davis says. "Now, running a dramatic production isn't only about acting on a stage. There's choreography, set design, lighting, music, understudies, tickets, and so much more. That said, some of you will do double duty. Some will be more behind the scenes, which is just as important. And with the play premiering on Halloween, we'll need to get to work right away! Are we ready to find out who our cast is for *Little Shop of Horrors*?"

We all start shouting again. And I don't know why, but I realize I want to hear my name called. I want it so badly, I stop breathing.

Mr. Davis begins by announcing the production crew: "Running sound, music, and lighting will be Ruby Valentin, Matthew Davis, and Navdeep Singh."

Navdeep turns to me, John, and Clairna and slaps us all high fives.

Still not breathing.

"For set design, we have . . . Nicholas Rocco . . . Clairna Joseph . . ." Suffocating in five, four, three . . . "and Annabelle Louis."

Clairna yelps and gives me a hug. I, Annabelle Louis, will design the set for *Little Shop of Horrors*! Mom and Dad are going to lose their minds!

Then Mr. Davis moves on to announce the acting roles. The roles of Crystal, Ronette, and Chiffon go to three of Rachael's friends, loyal subjects numbers one, two, and three. Mr. Mushnik will be played by Raheem Hannibal, and Bryan Tucker will play Orin, the dentist.

"Playing the lead of Seymour Krelborn is Johnathan Lopez!"

John squeezes my hand so hard I think he'll crush my bones.

"And the understudy for Seymour will be Navdeep Singh!"

Navdeep and John bump fists.

"And finally for our female lead, Audrey."

Everyone gets really quiet as the tension

builds, even though we already know who it is. . . .

"Rachael Myers!" Mr. Davis yells, and the crowd goes wild. "And the understudy for the role of Audrey . . . goes to Annabelle Louis!"

I'm sorry. What did he just say?

Silence. Then one clap (from John). Then another (Navdeep) and another (Clairna). And a few more claps, followed by whispers of: "Oh, that's the girl from Germany!"

Someone hand me a spatula to scoop my mouth off the floor! Did Mr. Davis really just choose me to be an understudy? For Audrey? I was awful yesterday!

Rachael turns around and says, "Congrats." But there's that eye-roll thing again.

I'm trying to stop the tears from welling up. I'm happy for Rachael (even with her rolling eyes), and scared for me, but can I also say, happy for me too?

That's when I realize that I'd been lying to myself. That I don't do drama. That I don't like it . . . or sports . . . or anything, really, that involves school. Because here I am, jumping up and down in my seat, happy, and not fake-happy, but real, live, I'm-going-to-be-in-a-play happy!

Could it be that maybe, just maybe, I'm starting to like this thing called drama?

And cue inner dialogue battle!

Annabelle: NOPE!

Daphne: LIAR!

4

NEW VLOG POST

Mom is already home by the time Dad and I arrive. I told him the news in the car and made him promise to keep his mouth shut so I could be the first to tell Mom.

"How did everything go?" Mom asks as she puts some groceries away.

I feel the heat rising up to my face. I can barely hold it in. "I got not one but two parts! I am going to design the set, and I'm understudy for the lead role."

Mom pulls me in for a squeeze, then we start jumping up and down together. Then she stops and pulls me back to take a look at me.

"Hmm . . . I thought you didn't do drama?" Mom says sarcastically.

"I'm just an understudy. I won't have to be on stage, at least, in front of all those people. Rachael will make sure she's in the spotlight no matter what."

Dad searches the cabinets for a pot, and I'm already drooling, thinking of what he'll make for dinner tonight.

"Speaking of people, have you seen the views now? Over five thousand and counting for sports and almost four thousand for school lunch! It doesn't look like it's slowing down. People want to know when you'll post your next video," Dad says.

A tiny part of me wonders what would've happened if I'd done better yesterday. Would *I* have gotten the lead role? How can I vlog about something I wanted to hate, but actually ended up sort of liking? And there goes my movie-making brain, with a voiceover that says: *Time for a retake.* I feel a new vlog coming, and this time it'll be just what the doctor ordered. But first . . . homework.

* * *

Boy was I wrong about Dad making dinner. Just when I was craving pasta Bolognese and garlic bread, Mom dashed my hopes and gave Dad a break.

Tonight's specialty? Hot dogs and beans. Yuck! Dad and I sit through dinner pretending like it's the best meal we've ever had. I am starting to get good at this acting thing!

After dinner I help Dad wash the dishes and then I steal away to my girl cave. The role of Audrey is calling me. This is my chance for a do-over—a chance to show what I would have done if I'd had my equipment with me. I sift through the racks of clothes and find *the* most perfect outfit for *Little Shop of Horrors*: a vintage-looking cream-colored dress with red roses and a short blond wig with baby-pink highlights. One coat of bright-red lipstick, and I am transformed into Audrey.

And lights, camera, action—and fake British accent!

"Hi, guys! It's your girl, Daphne. And I have a confession. My first video was called 'Daphne Definitely Doesn't Do Sports,' and in that video I talked about the top five reasons I think sports are simply dreadful. Because this channel is a social experiment, I was supposed to try new things that I might discover I like . . . such as sports. But we all know that was an epic fail. So yeah, I broke the rules. Sorry, Mum. But today I'll play nice and do what I was supposed to do all along. Today's episode is . . ."

And cue drumroll . . .

"'Daphne *Does* Drama'! So, it's no secret that I love movies. I make them, I dream of them, and sometimes when I'm feeling really creative, I'll act out a scene—even if it's mostly in my head. But it just so happens that I love *Little Shop of Horrors*! I mean, who doesn't? Set in the 1960s.

A bloodthirsty plant that snacks on humans to survive. There's singing, dancing, a budding romance. Pure perfection! So, ladies and gentlemen, playing the LEAD role of Audrey—it's *moi*, Daphne."

Insert loud applause.

I blow kisses to my imaginary adoring fans. "Oh, you guys are far too kind!"

I do away with my British accent and change my voice to make it squeaky like Audrey's. "This will be a reading of my favorite lines in the play." I take a deep breath, then begin my monologue: "I dream of a place where we could be together at last . . ."

When I'm done I take another bow, and the applause track plays again. Editing everything is super easy. I drop the clips in iMovie and throw in some cool transition tricks.

Just then Mae sends me a text with a picture of herself. Surprisingly, she's dressed in a wig and an over-the-top outfit.

Mae: You're going to be so popular,

girl, I'm dressing up as Daphne for Halloween!

Still dressed in my costume, I head to the bathroom upstairs while texting back.

Me: Mae, there's no Halloween in the UK.

Mae: Well, there will be after this. Just check your views, *amiga*!

I click on my YouTube channel, and oh my stars, my two vlogs now have a combined total of . . . 11,200 views!

I send Mae another text.

Me: Just uploaded a third video a few minutes ago. Take a look and let me know what you think.

I take off my wig, and it drops to the floor. But I'm way too tired to pick it up.

I send Mae a pic, holding up two fingers, for two *amigas*. She sends back a picture of herself doing the same.

Just like the script from *Little Shop of Horrors* says, *I dream of a place . . .*

I add my own words to that line . . . *a place where Mae and I could be together again.*

5

WANNABE

Mr. Davis wastes no time preparing us for the play. There's practice after school Monday through Thursday, two hours each day. Things are super busy these days, and I am finally starting to feel like I have a social life. Not to mention balancing homework and my vlog.

During rehearsal the past two days, Nicholas, Clairna, and I have assembled the stairs for the pet shop scene, colored in the floor tile paper, and painted the *Little Shop of Horrors* sign, complete with blood dripping from the letters. Today's project: tackling that overgrown, man-eating plant, Audrey II.

Mr. Davis runs lines with John and Rachael at center stage, while Mrs. Gironda reviews choreography with the rest of the cast. Even though we've only been practicing for two days, we're running like a well-oiled machine!

"Navdeep, Annabelle, stop what you're doing and run this same part." Mr. Davis has John and Rachael take a seat in the front row. This has been the norm. The actors rehearse their parts, and then Mr. Davis calls in the understudies to do the same.

Nav and I take our places at center stage. Nav holds the script, hands shaking, and looks at me with wide eyes.

"In three, two, one, action!" Mr. Davis yells out.

Nav begins reading from the script. When it's my turn to speak, I let the words flow naturally, picturing myself as Daphne, the fearless YouTuber.

When I finish my last line, Mr. Davis calls, "Cut!"

Everyone claps, and Nav and I take a bow.

"Excellent work! Annabelle, you already have the script memorized?" Mr. Davis asks.

"Yes, sir." I shift my eyes to Rachael and try to gauge the meaning of the look on her face.

Mr. Davis sends Nav back to the sound booth and me back onstage to help Clairna and Nicholas finish building Audrey II, the flesh-eating plant.

"Dude, that was amazing!" Nicholas says. "You could have totally played the lead role."

"Yeah!" Clairna chimes in.

"I don't know. I love what we're doing." The words feel stale coming out of my mouth. "This is more exciting, the behind-the-scenes stuff."

Do I really mean that, though? Because performing that scene for my vlog last night felt pretty darn amazing. Still, building the set is right up my alley. It's like re-creating my girl cave all over again, only on a bigger scale.

It's OK to like both, right? To secretly like the spotlight *and* create stage art with my hands?

And cue inner dialogue battle again!

Daphne: Of course it is!

Annabelle: Nope. Pick a team!

Clairna pulls out the green paint so we can color the large head of the plant. Just then someone's phone beeps. We all pause to listen if it's our phone.

"Whoops, that's me!" Nicholas pulls his iPhone out of his back pocket, swipes the screen, and his whole face lights up.

"What is it?" Clairna asks.

"That's weird," Nicholas begins. "Here we are running rehearsals for *Little Shop of Horrors*, and a video of that Daphne girl pops up and guess what she's performing?"

Clairna yanks the phone out of Nicholas's hand. "No way!"

I breathe in deep and then move next to Clairna to see.

"I'm telling you, sometimes I think the Internet is like, stalking our lives," Nicholas says.

Clairna clicks the play button, and we all watch together. There I am on the screen playing the role of Audrey, and here I am in real life dying faster by the second.

"Eh, I don't know about this one," Nicholas says. "Her sports video was a LOT funnier."

And cue speed-racing heartbeat!

Clairna throws in an extra blow. "Agreed. The lunch one too. This one's all serious and stuff."

Before I get a chance to throw in my bit—*well, I think this is pretty good, considering I'm the human version of a turtle!*—Mr. Davis catches us slacking off. He leaves John and Rachael and joins us near the overgrown plant. "Guys, we're supposed to be building a set, not playing on our phones."

"Sorry, Mr. Davis," Clairna says sincerely.

"It's just—there's this YouTuber who posted a video of herself performing a monologue from *Little Shop of Horrors*."

"Yeah, *ummm*, we *ummm*, wanted to show you how amazing it is!" Nicholas says.

Nicholas hands Mr. Davis the phone, and he presses play. Right away, Mr. Davis starts wrinkling his nose and twisting up his face.

That's when I know for sure my video stinks worse than Limburger cheese. (I love my German food, but that one's got to go!) It's not only his face that says it, it's the number of views: A whopping six! No comments? No shares?

And I posted it almost 24 hours ago! Mr. Davis watches to the end and then marches backstage with Nicholas' phone still in his hand.

"What is he doing?" I ask.

"Looks like somebody got jacked for his phone!" Clairna teases.

"Not funny, Clairna! I just got that for my birthday." Nicholas crosses his arms like a toddler.

Mr. Davis returns with a television on a cart with wheels, rolls it to center stage, and connects Nicholas' phone to the screen.

This isn't happening.

He clangs the bell, making everyone stop what they're doing. "Everyone, gather around," he says. "Take a seat in the first few rows."

This can't be happening.

The cast and crew fly to the seats. John beckons for me to sit next to him, which also happens to be beside Rachael.

"It seems that our set designers have found a lovely video of an actress performing a scene from our play. And I wanted to share it with you."

I whisper to no one in particular, "I didn't find anything! Leave me out of it!"

As soon as he presses play, every single body part of mine loses functionality. Any second now, I'm going to vomit. In three . . . two . . .

The video ends right before I spontaneously combust.

Everyone starts clapping. I feel Rachael's eyes on me. This is it. *She knows.*

I shift my gaze on her. Rachael whispers, "I've never even heard of that girl." The five-hundred-pound weight on my shoulders poofs away.

"This, dear cast, is commitment!" Mr. Davis is all riled up. "The characterization, the accent, it's flawless! We can all learn from this."

Mr. Davis seems to look at Rachael, and she sinks into the chair.

Meanwhile, I look around at the other kids and hear them whisper:

"What's the name of that YouTuber?"

"Oh, the I-hate-sports girl?"

"I liked the school lunches video better."

"OK, enough of the chit-chat, guys!" Mrs. Gironda, chief cell phone snatcher, yells out. "We have to finish up rehearsals."

"Yes, now run along! Back to work!" Mr. Davis shoos everyone off to their various locations in the auditorium.

John leans in to Rachael and me. "That was really good. She kind of reminded me of you, Annabelle. Right, Rachael?"

Before I can even answer, Rachael says, "I'm not going to take pointers from some *wannabe* YouTube star! You know what I'm saying?"

She looks straight at me.

On the inside, I feel myself breaking, piece by piece. That wannabe is me.

But I just nod, because I *think* that's what you do when the most popular girl in school offers you a breadcrumb of attention. Then I say, "You got that right, girl!"

6

DAPHNE DOES DRAMA

Nine views. Zero shares. Zero new subscribers.

I didn't think it could get much sadder than this. But then I saw the comment. Yup. Not plural. Just one:

TooCoolForSchool: Go back to your Daphne Doesn't format. Quick!

Point taken!

7

GROUP PROJECT

The next day Mr. Davis starts off history class with a special announcement. "This week we will focus on the Age of Exploration." He paces up and down the rows of seats. "Now, who can name some famous explorers?"

Nicholas raises his hand. "Ooh, Christopher Columbus!"

"Aka civilization destroyer," John blurts out, and the whole class laughs. John straightens his shoulders like he's proud of himself.

"There is truth to that, John," Mr. Davis says. "Christopher Columbus' expeditions ushered in a movement that began the transatlantic slave trade and wiped out millions of indigenous people."

I don't want to speak, I try not to speak, but ACK! This was Mae's and my favorite history topic, and I just have to say something! "Columbus wasn't the only one, though. There were other explorers before and after him."

The whole class is staring at me. Mr. Davis stops walking and leans back a bit. "Do tell, Miss Louis."

Oh dear. Here come the eyeballs. Lots of them. And they're all pointed at me. I clear my throat and try to block them out. "Well, there were several European countries that wanted to find new trading routes so they could discover new lands, silks, and spices. So people like Amerigo Vespucci and Marco Polo were responsible for enhanced methods of navigation and mapping, which sort of turned geography into science, and—"

"This ain't science class, girl!" Rachael says a little too loudly.

And cue laughter and not-so-whispery whispers!

"Annabelle is a real nerd."

"How does she know all that stuff?"

"Because she's not from this planet."

That last comment sends a cold shiver down my back.

"Settle down, everyone." Mr. Davis claps three times. "What a nice tie-in to this week's assignment, Annabelle!"

As soon as Mr. Davis turns his back and walks to the front of the room, John holds out his fist for me to bump it. Then Mr. Davis says two fatal words that remind me of reason number 391 why I never liked going to regular school: "group projects."

Note to self: Here's your next vlog! "Daphne Definitely Doesn't Do Group Projects."

For the two and a half years I went to school

in Spain, I would get stuck doing all the work. Every. Single. Time. By the time we moved to the UK, I was over it.

"OK, class, stand up and step away from your chairs," Mr. Davis orders. "Now, because I like to make things as democratic as possible, I'm going to give you exactly thirty seconds to create a group of three. In four . . . three . . ."

I can feel John's eyes piercing my skull, but he's not the only one.

"Two . . . one!"

John dashes to my side, and Rachael does a ballerina leap over her seat, knocking it over to join him. Two seconds ago she was making fun of me. And now here she is, clinging to my side like we're *amigas*.

Other kids are bum-rushing their way to get to our group.

"Don't even think about it!" Rachael warns.

A few sighs, followed by random mumbling. "Oh man, I wanted to be in Annabelle's group!"

The thirty-second time limit ends, and there are still a few stragglers walking around with disappointed faces. That doesn't stop Mr. Davis from reminding them they have no choice but to team up and make it work.

"Excellent!" he says once everyone has found a group. "Now, every group will pick out of a hat. Your card will have the name of the explorer you will research. You'll have a week to pull together your project. For the presentation, I'll let you decide how you will share your information. Act, sing, dance, make a Prezi—whatever you can creatively come up with."

Rachael picks out of the hat for us. "Amerigo Vest . . . poo . . ." she has a hard time getting the name out.

"Vespucci," I finish for her. "America's actually named after him."

"Guys, we're gonna need to set up some time after school to get this done," John says.

He's right. Between other homework, play rehearsals, and making Daphne videos, I'm definitely going to need some outside time to work on this.

"Good idea, but where?" Rachael asks. "Umm, we can't meet at my house because . . ."

"My house works!" The words come out so fast, they surprise me.

John shrugs and gives a nod. "Fine by me. When?"

"Let's shoot for tomorrow, after play practice," I say.

"OK, cool," Rachael says.

The bell rings, the classroom empties, and just like that it hits me: Tomorrow the most popular girl at McManus will hang out . . . with *me* . . . at my house.

8

CURRY AND CONVERSATION

Tonight's dinner scene is brought to you by spicy food and a spicy mood.

Going live in four, three, two, one . . .

ME

I have some friends coming over tomorrow after play practice. Can you pick us up at 4:30?

MOM

Oooh, *friends*—I like the sound of that!

Dr. Varma will too. Which reminds me, I need to
make another appointment soo—

DAD

(*cuts Mom off*)

Who exactly are these *friends*?

(*loosens tie around neck*)

ME

Rachael Myers and Johnathan Lopez.

We have a social studies project

to work on.

MOM

Ah, history was my favorite in middle school.

What topic?

ME

European Age of Exploration.

We're researching Amerigo Vespucci.

DAD

(*complexion deepens two shades*)

Is he ugly?

ME

Dad, all of those ancient explorer guys were
weird-looking, if you ask me.

Cue theme music for the movie Jaws.

DAD

(*half-choking on a chicken bone*)
The boy. Is the boy ugly?

*Zoom in on Mom laughing, me grabbing water
to mellow out Dad's famous curry chicken.*

ME

Um, no. Wait, I don't know. Maybe.
What kind of question is that?
(*morphs slowly into a glob*)

MOM

Aww, I think Annabelle has a little *novio*,
Ruben.

ME

Don't do that, Mom.
He's not my boyfriend.

DAD

(*transforms into a human habanero pepper*)

I'll pick you up from school, but I need parent phone numbers. You can work in the living room.

But he'd better be ugly.

End scene!

* * *

For the record, Johnathan Lopez is not ugly. He's . . . *OK* . . . I guess.

UGH!

9

A CONNECTION

When play practice is over, John, Rachael, and I walk out of the building just as Dad is pulling up.

We hop into Dad's black Equinox, and I'm praying he doesn't say or do anything to embarrass me. "Dad, this is John. John, my dad," I say. Dad's already met Rachael, since she showed me around McManus on my first day.

"Hello, Mr. Louis." Johnathan gives Dad a proper greeting, handshake and all.

"Nice to meet you," Dad says. "And good to see you again, Rachael. Buckle up, guys."

Dad turns on the radio, and Rachael immediately says, "Mr. Louis, can you turn it up? This is my song!"

Rachael is singing along and dancing in her seat. I start bopping my head up and down like I'm into it too. Dad throws me a smirk, almost like he gets it. Like he knows that this is what it takes to make friends.

Minutes later, we get to the house, and I tell Rachael and John to get set up in the dining room. The table is extra long, which will give us plenty of room to spread out our notes.

I walk into the kitchen and find Dad sitting at the breakfast bar, pretending to read the newspaper. But I know better. He keeps peeking out and staring at John.

"Dad, please don't be weird, OK?"

"I thought you were supposed to be making friends, like girl friends . . . not *boys*," he whispers.

I laugh and pat Dad on the shoulder. "It's just a school project. Relax."

I pull out a tray from the cabinet to make a quick snack. I line the tray with carrot sticks, hummus, trail mix, and chips. Then I grab a few water bottles from the fridge. As I walk out of the kitchen with my hands full, I notice the door to the basement is wide open. The lighted stairs are screaming, *Come on down!*

"Dad, please don't forget to close the door," I whisper.

"Why?" he asks. "You don't want them to see your awesome girl cave?"

His voice is almost a little too loud. I give him a Rachael-level eye roll. Code for: "I would die!"

Dad gets the message and closes the door as I walk into the dining room.

John and Rachael bum-rush me as soon as I get there. "Snacks!" they scream together.

This is what the next two hours look like: John reciting key points about Amerigo Vespucci's life and expeditions, me taking that information, adding my own notes, and typing it into the Prezi tool on my laptop. Rachael is paying us zero attention.

"Geez, girl." Rachael studies every picture hung on the walls of our living room and dining room. "How many places have you lived?"

"A lot." I keep typing, wondering when she'll actually join us to put in her two cents, but I don't say anything.

John doesn't bite his tongue. "Do you feel like joining in on the fun here, or what?" he asks, taking over my computer to type the next-to-last slide.

"Looks like you guys got it." Rachael brushes John off. "Just make sure you spell my name right. I can't stand it when I'm working in a group and they write my name wrong."

"Funny how you mentioned work, especially when you—"

"I'll just do it," I cut John off, grab the computer, and type all three of our names on the finished product.

Delicious smells from the kitchen begin to travel into the living room.

"What is your dad cooking in there?" John asks.

Nosey Dad, who apparently has been listening all along, yells out, "*Schnitzel*, with a Puerto Rican twist! You guys can stay for dinner if it's OK with your parents."

Please say yes, please say yes!

Just then, Rachael's phone buzzes in her pocket. "Oh shoot! It's already six o'clock. My mom's outside." She looks genuinely disappointed—or maybe I'm imagining it. "I'll take a rain check on that . . . what's it called again?"

"*Schnitzel*. We ate it a lot in Germany. It's like a breaded meat, and Dad makes rice, beans, and plantains to go with it." My stomach gives a roar of approval.

"See you at school, Rachael," John says, "Annabelle, where's the restroom?"

"Down the hall, first door on the right," I say, then I walk Rachael to the porch.

"I saw those pictures of your mom in her Air Force uniform," she says. "My dad's in the military too."

"You never mentioned that before. What branch?" I ask.

Rachael pulls two braids behind her ear. "Army."

"I bet my mom would love to meet him."

"Yeah, that probably won't happen for a while. He's been deployed for a year. Sometimes it feels like he's never coming home."

I know that feeling all too well, even though Mom's assignments have never lasted more than a couple of weeks.

For the first time, I see something different in Rachael. Not the flashy, diva, non-project-helping, popular Rachael I'm used to seeing at school. This one is open, vulnerable—but that only lasts for a split second. Rachael shakes it off and says, "Whatever. I'll see you tomorrow."

If I'm not mistaken, Rachael and I totally just

had "a moment." I might be making another friend at McManus. One who's got adoring fans and who "puts her face on," but one who also just might have some things in common with me. In my mind I take a picture so I can remember this.

Rachael's mom's car cruises off down Madison Street, and a white minivan pulls up out front immediately after.

"John, I think your ride is—" I can't finish the words because John is already behind me.

Giggling. And holding my wig. Yes, *that* wig. "I found this on the bathroom floor," he says.

Panic takes over. I snatch it from his hands.

"You know, your wig reminds me of that Daphne girl on YouTube."

I laugh a nervous, *get-out-of-here* laugh. "Oh yeah, I never noticed."

"Why do you have that? Got some secret identity I don't know about?" He winks.

I do a quick brain scan for a good lie. "No!" There's my fake laugh again. "It's part of my

Halloween costume." My shoulders lower half an inch.

John nods a believing *OK!*

Outside his *abuela* grows impatient and honks the horn. John grabs his backpack and starts walking down the stairs. Then he stops short and turns around.

"For what it's worth, I think you'd make the perfect Daphne for Halloween."

He throws me a smile, that left dimple sinking in all the way to his soul. And there I am, with my mouth slow-falling toward the steps, watching him walk to the car. John hops in the passenger seat, waves goodbye, and he and his grandmother drive off under a full moon while I stand there wondering, *What the heck just happened?*

10
LAST CALL

Things have been going beyond amazing at school. My grades are good (Mr. Davis gave us an A on the Amerigo Vespucci project). I have some cool friends: John, Clairna, Navdeep. Even Rachael talks to me a little—like in the halls passing by, never at lunch when she's at her diva table. But still, it's something.

And the best part of all is that after a few mix-ups and a couple of paper cuts, the set for *Little Shop of Horrors* is complete. Everyone knows their part. Tomorrow is the day we've all worked these few weeks for: showtime!

Because tomorrow is Halloween, Mr. Davis says that everyone on the stage crew can dress up in a costume of our choice.

Just as our final play rehearsal ends, I get a text.

Dad: Belle, going to be five minutes late.

Me: OK, I'll hang here. Text me when you're outside.

Everyone has gone home, and the auditorium is empty.

"Should I call your parents?" Mr. Davis asks.

I tell him Dad is running late.

"I have to print out the programs for the show," he says. "I'll be in the office. Just pop in and let me know when you're leaving."

"OK," I say.

As soon as the door swings shut behind Mr. Davis, I step onstage and take it all in. The lights, the set that I helped design. Everything is perfect. I don't know what takes over me, but I start reciting my favorite part of the play, just like I did on my vlog, but this time even better.

"I don't believe this!"

I press the remote to make the man-eating plant, Audrey II, move her lips.

"Believe it, baby! I can talk!" Audrey II screams.

"Am I dreaming right now?" I place my hand on my chest, exhale dramatically, and take a bow.

A slow clap rings out from the audience. At first I think it's Mr. Davis, but as the shadowy figure walks down the aisle, I realize it's not.

"By all means, continue acting out *my* part." Rachael crosses her arms tightly.

Horror finds its way to my face. "Sorry, I was just fooling around. I didn't mean to—"

"Steal my shine?"

OUCH!

"Anyway, I forgot my notebook." Rachael places her fist over her mouth and lets out a liquidy-sounding cough.

"Of course, you do the scene better," I say. I die a little more after each word.

"Whatever. I get it." Rachael coughs again. "That's one of my favorite scenes too." She finds her notebook, places it in her backpack, and then starts to walk away.

Everything inside of me is crumbling into dust.

"You know," Rachael says as she turns around, "if you weren't so . . . I don't know . . . *different*, I'd say judging by the way you just performed, you were the real Daphne."

Different. Translation: dorky.

The imaginary camera pulls in tight to my face. *Hello, sweat beads!*

"Not that I watch that or anything," she says flatly.

"Yeah, me neither," I lie. My shoulders collapse into my chest.

"And girl, I was just kidding."

I shrug. "Yeah, totally."

And end scene!

11

IT'S SHOWTIME!

On the opening night of the show, I get a text.

Mae: Good luck tonight. I wish I could be there, but will be rooting for you from across the pond!

Mom helps me dress up as jazz legend Billie Holiday for Halloween. It's totally different from how I typically dress at school, which according to Rachael is *different*, aka dorky. But tonight Mom transforms me into a celebrity. She pulls my curly hair into a low bun. For once, every strand feels like it's in place. She sprays it with hair spray just to make sure. She gives me one of her dresses to wear. Navy blue velvet with a white flower attached to the lapel. And to top it off, a white flower for my hair.

"You look beautiful," Dad says as I come down the stairs.

We drive to McManus, and when we get there the parking lot is packed. It seems like all of Linden showed up to support us on opening night!

"See you after the show!" I kiss Mom and Dad goodbye.

When I walk backstage, I get stares from Navdeep and John.

"Um, hi, Annabelle!" Nav says, his cheeks growing red.

Then John goes, "This costume's even cooler than the Daphne one!"

Before I respond, they both whip around so fast, as if it was choreographed.

Boys can be so weird sometimes!

After that, a few of the cast members and backstage crew start complimenting me.

"Awesome costume!"

"Who are you dressed up as?"

"Duh, she's that singer lady from the old days!"

"Well, well, well, look who decided to dress normal," Rachael says. She is seated at a lighted table with a mirror, guzzling something from a thermos. Her skin looks damp and a little grayish-green. Not her typical golden brown.

"Are you OK, Rachael?" I ask, walking over to her.

"Just a tickle in my throat." She sighs. "And I wish my parents were in the audience. But, whatever. Work comes first. Always."

Rachael begins to *put her face on*, and I'm sure I see tears building up in her eyes. I lean over and give her a hug. She doesn't hug me back though. In fact, she kind of pushes me away.

"I'll be all right," she says.

Mr. Davis yells for us to take our spots because the show is about to begin!

The character trio of Crystal, Ronette, and Chiffon take their places in front of the closed curtains. The music begins, and they belt out the signature song, "Little Shop of Horrors."

Halfway through the song, the curtains open, revealing the shop in all of its glory. The audience erupts in applause and then settles down as the actors begin their lines.

Rachael, as Audrey, enters stage left, while John, aka Seymour, makes loud noises behind the set. John enters the stage, clumsily tripping over his own feet, causing a roar of laughter from the audience.

The story moves through the lives of Mr. Mushnik, the unhappy owner of a failing flower shop, Seymour, an orphan who's totally crushing on Audrey, and then there's Audrey, an urban girl with suburban dreams.

The discovery of a Venus flytrap–looking plant gives them all the kind of hope they need.

The music cues up for "Somewhere That's Green."

Rachael begins singing, "I know he is the greatest!" The first notes come out in perfect pitch.

I stand in the wings, mouthing each word she sings.

But then: ". . . still" (*cough*) "Seymour's" (*cough*) "a" (*cough, cough*) "cutie!"

"What's up with Rachael's voice?" Clairna whispers in my ear.

I don't know why, but my nerves take over. And I'm not the one on stage. On the inside, I'm whispering to Rachael, *Take a deep breath! You got this!*

But that doesn't stop her downward spiral until the final note.

The curtains close. Clairna, Nicholas, and I change the set for the next scene. Meanwhile, I hand Rachael a bottle of water and a paper towel to wipe her drenched face. Once the curtains open again for the next-to-last scene of

Act 1 (feeding Audrey's wackadoodle boyfriend to the overgrown fly trap), Rachael's face turns paler than her blond wig.

She makes it through once more, coughing after every word. It's during intermission when the chaos begins. Clairna and I close the curtains. Rachael makes a beeline toward the garbage can near the stage exit door. She trips a bit, almost misses it, but gets there just in time to empty out the contents of her stomach.

We all rush to her side.

"Are you sick?" someone asks.

I pat her on the back, helping her get the rest out, holding my breath to block out the smell. Rachael lifts her colorless, sweaty face and says, "I don't feel so good. Can we just extend intermission another few—"

Rachael starts throwing up all over again.

Mr. Davis is panicking now. "Rachael's family in the audience! Find them, NOW!" he shouts. "Annabelle, we need you to take over her part!"

Now I feel like *I'm* the one who's going to throw up!

"Absolutely not!" Rachael pipes up. "I didn't work this hard to let her take my spot!" She wipes her mouth with the sleeve of her dress. "I just need about ten more minutes."

Rachael's grandfather arrives backstage with a bottle of ginger ale and a plastic bag. "Her mom had to work late tonight. I'll take it from here," he tells Mr. Davis.

The next thing I know, Mrs. Gironda is shuffling up to me, waving a black leather bag full of props. "Clairna, quick! Help me get Annabelle changed."

The two of them swish me away from the scene to a room backstage. Mrs. Gironda locks the door.

"What's happening here?" I'm so confused.

Neither of them answer. Mrs. Gironda goes into action mode. She tosses Clairna the Audrey wig and makeup bag and orders her to *put my face on*. Clairna starts piling the stuff on like I'm a cake being frosted. Mrs. Gironda hands me a leotard.

"And when you're done, spray this on your bottom," she says.

I move the bottle closer to my face and notice the name: BUTT SPRAY.

"What in the world is this?" I can't hold in my confusion.

"A theater essential, my dear," Mrs. Gironda says. "It'll keep the leotard in place."

Clairna laughs. "Aka wedgie blocker!"

Everything is moving too fast. Mrs. Gironda attaches a body mic to the collar of my dress, unlocks the door, and starts pushing me toward the stage. I don't even have time to say no. "Whew! Perfect timing!" she says. "Intermission is almost over."

The heavy curtains smack me in the face, leaving a tiny opening. The houselights are still up, and everyone is going back to their seats. I spot Mom and Dad making their way down the aisle. When those curtains finally open, I'm not sure which of us will be the first to have a heart attack.

Clairna and Nicholas roll in a second version of Audrey II, the biggest model we created for the set.

"We're ready to begin the second act. Quiet on set! Places, everyone!" Mr. Davis whispers.

Clairna gives me a fist bump before rushing to the side of the curtains.

Mr. Mushnik, Ronette, and I position ourselves at the phones, ready to receive the thousands of calls that are coming in, all thanks to our main attraction, Audrey II.

My pulse is on high speed, mind scattering to remember the lines. The music cues up. The stage lights rise. I want to crumble right there in the middle of the stage. Or run away and never come back again. But then I see Mom and Dad. And as soon as they see me, Mom starts slapping Dad on the shoulder.

Code for: "Holy moly, Ruben, get your camera out! Our baby is up there!"

I take a deep breath, and suddenly I don't feel so afraid. In my mind, it's just me up there, pretending to be someone I am not. Just like Daphne.

The phones begin to ring off the hook, and the three of us talk over each other.

"Thank you for calling Mushnik and Son. Your favorite florists of Skid Row!"

And I soar like this right through to the end. Never missing a beat, a note, or a line.

When the play is over, we all line up backstage behind the closed curtains, and I hear the whispers.

"Good job, Annabelle!"

"That was amazing!"

I grow taller with every word. The curtains open, and the crowd goes wild.

One by one, Mr. Davis calls the cast members forward. He announces that Rachael Myers played the role of Audrey for the first act, and saves John and me for last. John reaches out to take my hand and winks at me. My stomach does this flippy-floppy thing as I see the spotlight twinkle in his brown eyes.

As soon as the curtains close, everyone scrambles to find their parents. I don't have to look very far. Mom and Dad are waiting at the foot of the stage with flowers.

Mom elbows me in the side when I get to her, "Well, that was quite the surprise! Nice work, sweetie!"

"Yes, you were a real professional up there." Dad kisses me on the forehead.

"Thank you, Mom, Dad." I lean in to my dad's embrace, feeling my whole universe warm up.

"Why don't you grab the rest of your things and we'll meet you at the car? K, *Daph*?" Mom winks at me, and she and Dad make their way toward the exit.

When I turn around, Rachael Myers is standing smack in front of me. Empty barf bag in her hand. Her face a little less green.

"Whoa, you scared me! I thought you went home," I say.

"Did your mom just call you *Daph* . . . as in Daphne?"

"How are you feeling?" I ask Rachael.

"Way to avoid the question, Annabelle." She does her signature arm-cross move, though the barf bag makes her look borderline ridiculous.

I squirm a little but keep my cool. "Oh that? Noooo, my mom said I made her *laugh*—not Daph!"

"I heard what I heard." Rachael doesn't flinch. Then she eyeballs me up and down. "I begged my grandpa to let me stay and see the rest of the play. Hope you enjoyed your little moment. It wouldn't have happened if I didn't get sick."

She starts coughing, spit flying, germs dancing in the air. I take a step back.

"I hope you feel better, Rachael."

"I'm sure you do," Rachael says. Then she walks away, holding on to that empty barf bag as if her life depended on it.

12

I DON'T DO DRAMA

When I get home, I retreat to my girl cave, because even though I should feel on top of the world right now, I don't. I don't want to talk to Mom or Dad. Or even Mae. She texts me around ten p.m., which means it's three in the morning in the UK, which means she literally waited up all night to ask: "Hey, *amiga*! How was the play?"

And for once, I don't respond. I know, I know. Worst. Friend. Ever.

But I need time to sort through my feelings. I don't understand why Rachael seemed so mad at me. I only did what understudies are supposed to do—to step in when I was needed. At first I thought I would like doing drama, but what I'm seeing is that with drama comes "drama-drama," and that is not for me. Suddenly I feel an itch to make a video.

I look at my clothes rack and pick out an outfit—a royal, Victorian dress. I put on a white wig styled in a bouffant, piled high on my head, and bright-red lipstick. I hold a lace handkerchief in one hand for dramatic effect. I set up my camera and scribble down my scenes. A few runs through my lines, and I'm ready to shoot. Counting down in five, four, three, two . . .

"Hey, guys. It's your girl, Daphne, and I'm back with another episode of *Daphne Doesn't*. Now I know in my last video I was all about 'Daphne Does Drama.' But I changed my mind about one thing. I may like drama, but I definitely don't *do* drama, and here's why:

"Number one: Too much makeup. Like, seriously . . . how is it comfortable to walk around with an entire cake frosted on your face?

"Number two: The bright lights blinding you. It's like: Is the white light coming to get me? Is this how it all ends?

"Number three: Eyeballs. Yup, you heard that right. EYES, people!!! When you're on stage, there are people . . . staring at you. And then your heart starts to beat really fast and your hands start to sweat and you try to do what all the books say: Picture everyone in their underwear. But when you do that, you see your grandma sitting in the front row, and she's got hair on her chest. So you try to unsee that whole travesty, but when you do, it's back to the glowing eyeballs. And the fear starts all over again.

"Now I know what you're thinking: 'But Daphne, there are eyeballs watching you on these videos.' Touché! But! Right now it's just me in my girl cave, with a single camera. The eyeballs come later—when I'm not around. Whew! I've said a mouthful. But seriously, people: Beware the eyeballs.

"Number four: Butt spray. 'What is *that*?' you ask. I'm glad you did. Citizens of YouTube, there is a thing called butt spray, and if you can't already tell by the name, it's an adhesive that you spray . . . on your butt . . . to avoid getting a serious case of the wedgies mid-scene. So here you are walking around in your costume like one big sticky-butt zombie. And if you think that stuff comes off easily in the shower, think again. I still have spray in places I'd rather not mention.

"Number five: And last but not least, I definitely don't do drama because, well, I don't do the *other* kind of drama. The catty fighting over roles. This one is better than that one, etc. It's all just . . . exhausting. It's good to do theater if you want to learn how to be a good actress, but, dear listeners, don't *become* the drama, if you know what I mean. Want to know why? Because in the end there's enough sun for us all to shine.

"That's all for now! Share, like, comment, subscribe. However you're feeling, just go with it!"

13

DAPHNE CLIMBING

19,079 views. 1,850 shares. 3,714 subscribers.
I present a sample of the comments. . . .
Drumroll, please!

BritishBabe: Loving this funny girl! Just cheeky!

ThespianGoddess: Haters gonna hate. Keep doing your thing.

FamousLamous: Def keep the Daphne

Doesn't format. Loved the Group Project vlog, too, but this one is a slam dunk.

MaeFromTheUK: My bestie "Daphne" is going VIRAL! Don't get too famous on me, Jersey girl!

Ladies and gentlemen, I believe we're back on track.

14

MAKING THE DEAL

"I see your videos are really picking up steam," Dr. Varma says as I follow her into her office. "I showed the one you did about group projects to my daughter and we were cracking up. I'm telling you, Daphne will be viral before you know it."

Do I want to go viral? I'm not so sure.

I take a seat on her couch, and we begin our session.

"Tell me about your experience at McManus so far," she says.

"As you know, I've made some friends. John is really cool. Clairna and Navdeep are too. And then there's Rachael. Sometimes I don't think I have a lot in common with her. But then I learned something about her that made me think maybe I do."

"And what was that?"

"Her dad is in the military, like my mom. But he's been deployed."

"Well that certainly is a connection."

"He's been gone a year. And I'm starting to wonder if that has anything to do with the way she acts."

"How so?"

"One minute she's half-nice to me. She even came to my house, and she and John and I worked on a presentation together. Well, more like John and I did the work, and she sort of slacked off. But we still got an A on the project, so I guess it all worked out. But then she totally got mad at me over the play, even though she's the one who got sick and couldn't finish her part. I was just doing what I was supposed to do . . . fill in!"

"What do you feel is the source of her wishy-washy behavior?"

"I think maybe it's because she's missing her dad." I get really quiet after that. There's a ball slowly growing in my throat. Am I about to cry? Over Rachael's dad? Or is this about something more personal?

"Will the same thing happen to me . . . when Mom leaves?" I ask.

Dr. Varma leans forward and touches my hand. "We all react differently when it comes to being away from our parents. I think it's good that you acknowledge what Rachael is going through. It's probably an even better reason to connect with her. She might benefit from being around someone who understands. Have you told her about your mum's TDY?"

"No, I'm actually trying not to think about it," I say.

"Well, it is November," Dr. Varma says. "The

holidays will come fast, Annabelle. I'd say it's time for you to let your friends know. Along with your father, they will be your greatest support system. Also, you have me. I'll still be around." She pauses. "How are you holding up on the Daphne end?"

"I'm starting to feel like it's hard to keep it a secret. I almost got caught a couple of times."

Dr. Varma's eyes widen. "Tell me about it."

I tell her about how John asked to use the restroom at our house and found one of my Daphne wigs in there. And then how after the play, Rachael heard Mom call me "Daph," even though I denied it.

"Well that was a close one, wasn't it?"

I nod.

"You know, I have seen you blossom since you first started coming here."

"You have?"

"Oh, yes. You walk with a little more pride in your step. You're certainly less shy. And look, you even have some new friends. And even though things seem strained with Rachael, I think you might have a chance at a real connection with that one."

I smile. It's not like I want to be best friends with Rachael or anything. My best friend is Mae, and even though she's miles away, that will never change.

"So since you already discovered that you don't like sports and you do like drama, but you definitely don't like drama-drama. Let's figure out something else you can vlog about that you might enjoy. Maybe you can tell me what you're thinking."

"Well on the night of the play I dressed up nicely for once. And I don't mean like the over-the-top outfits I wear for my vlog. I mean like a real dress with my hair styled in a way that didn't make me look like a human oak tree. And for that one night I felt, I don't know . . . noticed. But in a good way. Even Rachael said I looked nice. And that girl is like the QUEEN of fashion at McManus."

I can see the light bulb switch on over Dr. Varma's head. "So what you're telling me is you might want to consider changing your wardrobe?"

"Yes. Well, no. Ugh!" My body deflates, and I become one with the couch. "Here's the thing—I like the way I dress. But I also liked the attention I got at the play. It was nice to not be so dorky for a change."

"Define dork," Dr. Varma says.

I run my fingers from the top of my head to the bottom of my shoes, indicating the definition is me.

Dr. Varma smiles. "There's nothing wrong with being a dork. Some of the brightest people call themselves dorks. But I do understand liking the feeling you had when you dressed up. So let's say we title your next vlog as 'Daphne Does Fashion.' It has a nice ring to it, doesn't it?"

I think about that for a moment. And then my internal movie starts up. My perfectly styled hair is blowing in the gentle wind. I'm wearing high leather boots, a cute pleated skirt, and a blazer. People are clapping as I enter the school building. I'm signing autographs and saying words like "darling" and "faaaaaabulous." And this time there is no storm or alarm clock to chase the image away.

I want to have a real moment like that. I can totally do this, with my fashionista mom's help.

"I like it, Dr. Varma," I say. "You've got a deal!"

TALK ABOUT IT!

1. Annabelle thinks she did awful in tryouts for the play, but is cast as understudy for the main role. Have you ever felt you've done poorly at something when you actually did well? Did you feel similarly to Annabelle when she found out she was cast in the play?

2. Rachael goes back and forth from seeming like Annabelle's friend to being cold to her. Dr. Varma describes the way Rachael treats Annabelle as "wishy-washy." Why do you think Rachael acts the way she does to Annabelle?

3. John and Rachael both nearly find out that Annabelle is Daphne when they visit her house. What do you think would have happened if they went downstairs and found the Daphne set?

WRITE IT DOWN!

1. Over the course of the story, Annabelle learns how hard it can be confronting negative thoughts, from her new video not getting many views to her lack of confidence in her acting. Write down some strategies you could use to fight against negative thoughts.

2. Annabelle's *Daphne Doesn't* videos are loved for her hilarious takes on school life. Pick a topic and write a script for a vlog of your own.

3. Annabelle isn't sure which role she'd like better in a play—being on stage and acting, or working backstage. Write a paragraph about which one you think you would like better.

ABOUT THE AUTHOR

Tami Charles writes picture books, middle grade and young adult fiction, and nonfiction. Her middle grade novel debut, *Like Vanessa*, is a Junior Library Guild selection. *Like Vanessa* was also selected by the American Bookseller's Association for the Indies Introduce Kids List. Tami is the author of four more books forthcoming with Albert Whitman & Co., Candlewick, and Charlesbridge. She resides in New Jersey with her husband and son.